Reading, writing, and art are key
to communicating our passions with others.

This book is for everyone who has a passion to share.

King for a Day
the Story of Stories

Written & Illustrated by Mark Wayne Adams

Published by:

CABALLOBOOKS

Contact Information:
Caballo Books
P.O. Box 916392
Longwood, FL 32791-6392

Author/Illustrator/Designer: Mark Wayne Adams
Editor: Jennifer Thomas

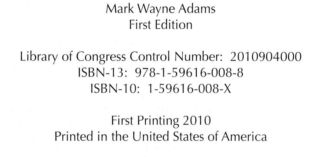

Mark Wayne Adams
First Edition

Library of Congress Control Number: 2010904000
ISBN-13: 978-1-59616-008-8
ISBN-10: 1-59616-008-X

First Printing 2010
Printed in the United States of America

Foreword

I was once like many of you: I wanted to *be* something. However, I had no clue what that might be. Other kids my age wanted to be doctors, athletes, and president. I wanted to draw.

I remember watching Walt Disney's *Fantasia* at age five. Right then, I realized that what I wanted was possible.

Many times, people tried to discourage my drawing dream. As I grew older, I learned to listen to the positive influence of people who told me I could. These people taught me to listen and to learn. I found many answers and kept notes along the way. Observing others meant it was possible for me.

King for a Day is a wonderful adventure about discovering your passion through friends and actions. I wrote this story to let young readers know how I do what I do, and to encourage them to create their own stories using the tools within themselves.

Have you ever wanted to change an ordinary day into an extraordinary story?

Well, first you must find your life's passion!

2

A passion is not a place or a thing.
It is an action—
an action that makes you happy.

3

My name is Russell. And I have many passions.
Playing, running, and telling stories are just a few.

What might your passions be?

4

I share my passions with my pals:
Carter, my best friend; Litto, my stuffed lion;
and Uma, my toy unicorn.

DRAGON WINGS

5

We spend our days together on Parsons Farm.
It is a magical place where most anything can happen.

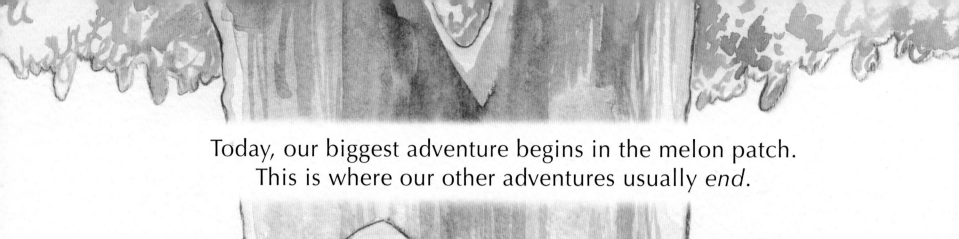

Today, our biggest adventure begins in the melon patch.
This is where our other adventures usually *end*.

7

The day began with Mom's note:

Since you don't have a story for the Jamboree,
please pick a melon to share for dessert.
I will meet you there.

   —Love, Mom

Today is Momma Gi Gi's Jamboree.
Today she will crown the best storyteller
"King for a Day."

Her unique invitation was a black journal
containing a puzzling message:

The greatest treasure is your story.
What role will YOU play?

Please share your story with me!

—Momma Gi Gi

10

CLIFTY CREEK BRIDGE

I must admit, however, that those are still
the only words in our book.
For two weeks, Carter and I have played
and have not written a word.

Now all we will have to offer is a melon
and Gi Gi's blank journal!

11

"I so wanted Gi Gi's crown," says Carter, sitting in the Parsons' empty wheelbarrow.

He reads Gi Gi's message once more and sighs. "Nothing in this melon patch is going to make either of us King for a Day."

12

Determined to cheer up my loyal friend,
I fashion a crown from the crumpled note,

"BARK! BARK! BARK!"
Here ye, here ye! I, hereby dub thee
King of the Melon Patch.

I place the crown upon his head.

13

"This is a wonderful crown!" Carter cheers.
"You are a true friend. Do I look like a king?"

"BARK! BARK!"
It looks GGGGRRREAT!

"BARK!"
Now, let's get rolling!

14

Carter and I select the largest, juiciest,
ripest melons we can find.
We merrily march our prizes to the edge of the patch.

Just beyond the patch fence, we see two
familiar friends enjoying an afternoon snack.

One looks much like Litto. The other favors Uma.
This can't be! Both are just toys.
We crouch down to listen.

"Pass me the treats and pour me another, Uma," growls the lion, adjusting himself upon a large melon.

"Litto," replies the unicorn,
removing the napkin from his knee.
"Aren't you eating more than your share?"

"Lions are agile and strong!" roars Litto.
"I need more food than you
to keep up my strength, you whimsical beast!"
His voice shakes the leaves in the tree above.

19

As the leaves settle, Uma catches sight of a magnificent treasure: a fantastic crown sitting upon a small, brownish melon—which is actually Carter's head.

Slyly, Uma grins.
"Litto, I was rude. You *are* agile and strong.
And I bet you are fast as well.
Run and fetch the Unicorn King his crown."
Uma points at us.

21

"Whoa, unicorn! You are no king!" Litto leaps from his seat, toppling his fresh glass of melon juice. "The King of the Jungle deserves that crown!"

Litto nods his head with conceit and bounds our way!

22

"Wait!" Carter puts out his hands.
"I am King of the Melon Patch! This is *my* crown."

Today may be Carter's last show of courage,
I write in the journal.
He shouldn't argue with a lion.

Litto and Uma shoot each other a look.
"It's *true* that he who wears the crown is king…" Uma begins.
"…but," Litto continues, "every king must *fight* to keep his crown."

Litto snatches the crown from Carter's head and in a flash, Litto, Uma, and the crown are headed toward town.

"Stealing my crown won't make you king!" Carter yells to the thieves.

"BARK! BARK!"
Let's stop them before they ruin the day!

I grab our journal, and away we go!

Along the path,
through a lovely garden...

26

...down a hill...

27

...over a wall...

28

...into a house...

and back out...

...ending at the bridge,
where Litto and Uma make a huge
splash!

30

I watch my beautiful crown disintegrate in the water.
Now, neither king has a crown—only his greed.

I offer up the journal as food for thought.
Carter again reads Gi Gi's message aloud:

"The greatest treasure is your story. What role will YOU play?"

32

The roles Litto and Uma played
in *their* story made them fools today.

Both leave town with heavy hearts
and an understanding of what does—
and doesn't—make a king.

PEEP!
PEEP!

Carter and I flop down on a hollow log and watch a parade of ants. As the sun begins to set, Carter sighs again.

"We wanted to be King for a Day, and now we have no crown, no melon, and no story. What will we do?"

34

"BARK! BARK! BARK!"
I think the answer is in front of us.

I nudge the journal with my nose.

"Come on!" Carter leaps up.
"We must hurry to the Jamboree!"

"Where have you been?!" exclaims Mom.
"You made it not a moment too soon."

"Where should we begin?" Carter winks
as I open our journal.

36

"Once upon a time," reads Carter, "we changed an ordinary day into an extraordinary story…"

The crowd listens quietly, only stirring to oooh and ahhh.

When our story of stories ends,
we are treated to thunderous applause!

This year, Gi Gi's Jamboree found her not *one*,
but *two* Kings for a Day!

39

Carter and I both agree:
*"The greatest treasure is your story…
and the role YOU play!"*

"BARK! BARK!"
*Our passion is more fun
than wearing a crown!*

40

Create Your Own Story

With these simple exercises, you, too, can write some fun into your life!

Step 1: Acquire your storytelling tools

To create your own story, you need only two things: (1) Something to write *with* (a pen, a pencil, or even a crayon!) and (2) Something to write *on*.

You may even want to ask your parents for a journal, sketchbook, or notebook to hold all your stories. Don't forget to sign your name in the front, so that if you lose it, it can be returned to you.

Remember: Never write or draw anything that you would not share with your parents. Your name is the most important thing you own. Don't diminish your name with offensive drawings or harsh words.

Carry your storytelling tools in your backpack or with you everywhere. You never know where your next idea will be found!

Step 2: Write your story

To become a great storyteller, you need to learn the basic parts of a story. Let's step through them as you create your own story.

The Setting

The location of your story has a big impact! Is it in the mountains, on a beach, or maybe in a melon patch? Is it the snowy dead of winter or a bright spring day? Describe your setting as fully as you can, so readers can imagine themselves in your story or picture.

The Characters

Define a character or set of characters who are unique to your story and who your readers will relate to. For example, if you like lizards and all your friends like lizards, then you'll probably do really well telling stories with lizards in them.

Ask yourself:
- Who is your main character? What makes him or her special?
- Who are the main character's supporting characters and friends?
- Will your story have a villain? Describe him or her.

Throughout your story, give your characters as much personality as you can. The better your readers can imagine them, the more they'll enjoy the story.

Special note: You also must decide who is telling the story. Is one of the characters telling the story—like Russell did? Or are *you* the narrator, telling the reader what happens to your characters?

The Goal

Your characters must have a purpose. Describe the main activity your characters are performing when the story begins. Do they have a specific goal they are trying to achieve?

The Problem

What problem do your characters encounter? Maybe it's some obstacle to meeting their goal, or a dangerous situation they must get through. Creating a meaningful challenge for your characters is crucial to creating a good story.

Rising Action

Describe everything that happens as your characters work toward overcoming their problem or reaching their goal.

The Climax

This is the high point of your story, where everything comes together. Maybe your characters encounter the villain, or must race against the clock to finish something in time. Make this part as dramatic as possible.

The Resolution

This is the end of the story, where everything works out one way or the other. Hopefully, the good characters achieve their goal and the bad characters are taught a lesson. Describe what happens.

Fun and Easy Quiz

Let's examine King for a Day using our story elements!

1. Who are the main characters?
2. What is the setting?
3. What is the goal of the main characters?
4. What problems do the main characters encounter?
5. What is the rising action?
6. What is the climax?
7. How is the story resolved?

7. *Carter reads Russell's story about their encounter with the thieves, and the pair are both crowned King for a Day. They learn that "The greatest treasure is your story."*

Drawing Lesson

Now that you have expressed your story through words, bring your story to life by adding illustrations! This lesson will show you how to express your story through shapes, layouts, and characters.

Find your inspiration

Before you begin drawing, it helps to become inspired. Here are my three favorite ways to find drawing inspiration:

Tip 1: Look at shapes in the grain of wood, stuccoed concrete, marble floors, or even the clouds above. Observing will help when you need a drawing idea.

Tip 2: Visit the drawing and picture book sections of your local library or bookstore. Find which illustrative styles you like and don't like.

Tip 3: Draw in an environment that inspires you. If being outside is your passion, create a comfortable place outside to draw, perhaps on a blanket under a tree or sitting in a chair on your patio.

Shapes

Can you draw the shapes above? Can you draw even more shapes? You will discover that these basic shapes can be used to create your own illustrations!

Exercise 1: Draw each of the above shapes five times in your sketch book. Practicing these shapes is important to understanding the construction of a page layout and a character.

Exercise 2: Examine how Carter was created from these basic shapes. Next, examine some other layouts and characters throughout this book. Can you see how shapes were used to create them?

Exercise 3: Note how Carter fits within a circle. You will be using different outer shapes and sizes to define the size and placement of each character and object within your page layout.

Layout Sketches

Before attempting to draw characters, practice your understanding of page construction. Shapes and lines form the structure of a book page. Shapes are used to place and create objects on the page. Lines represent movement or body position. Note that each page must also include a blank area in which to place story text.

Below is an example of the layout sketch used to create the illustration below. Basic shapes and lines are represented in pink over the illustrated page.

Story text!

Story text!

Exercise 4: Examine some other page layouts throughout this book. Can you see how shapes were used to create them?

Exercise 5: Using your sketchbook, start to recreate layouts from this book. Practice using shapes to determine the size and placement of objects and characters on the page. You will learn to draw these characters in the next section.

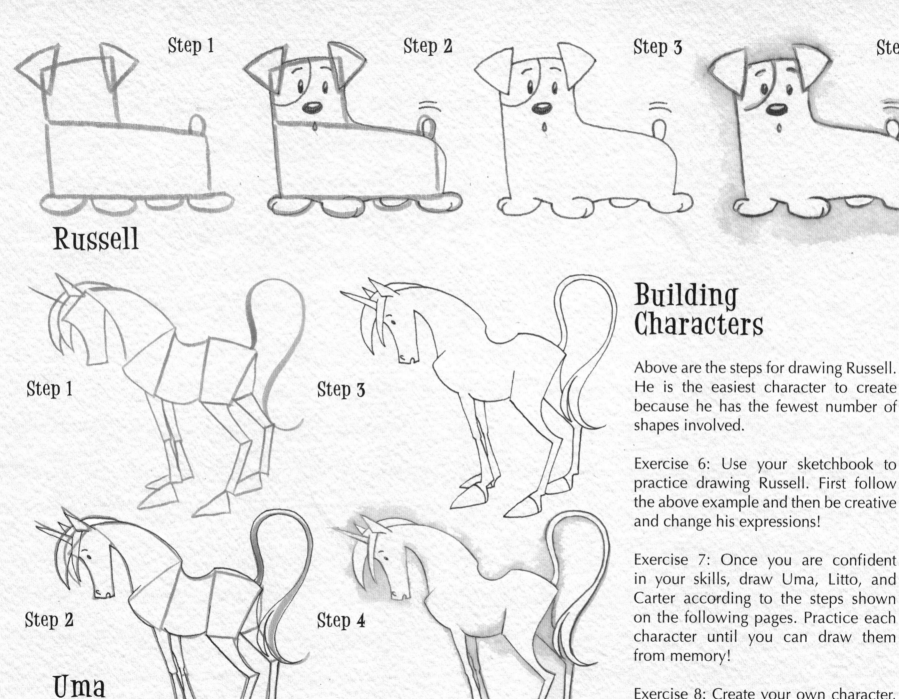

Step 1   Step 2   Step 3   Step 4

Russell

Step 1   Step 3

Step 2   Step 4

Uma

Building Characters

Above are the steps for drawing Russell. He is the easiest character to create because he has the fewest number of shapes involved.

Exercise 6: Use your sketchbook to practice drawing Russell. First follow the above example and then be creative and change his expressions!

Exercise 7: Once you are confident in your skills, draw Uma, Litto, and Carter according to the steps shown on the following pages. Practice each character until you can draw them from memory!

Exercise 8: Create your own character, using shapes to build it. Using shapes will help keep the character consistent.

45

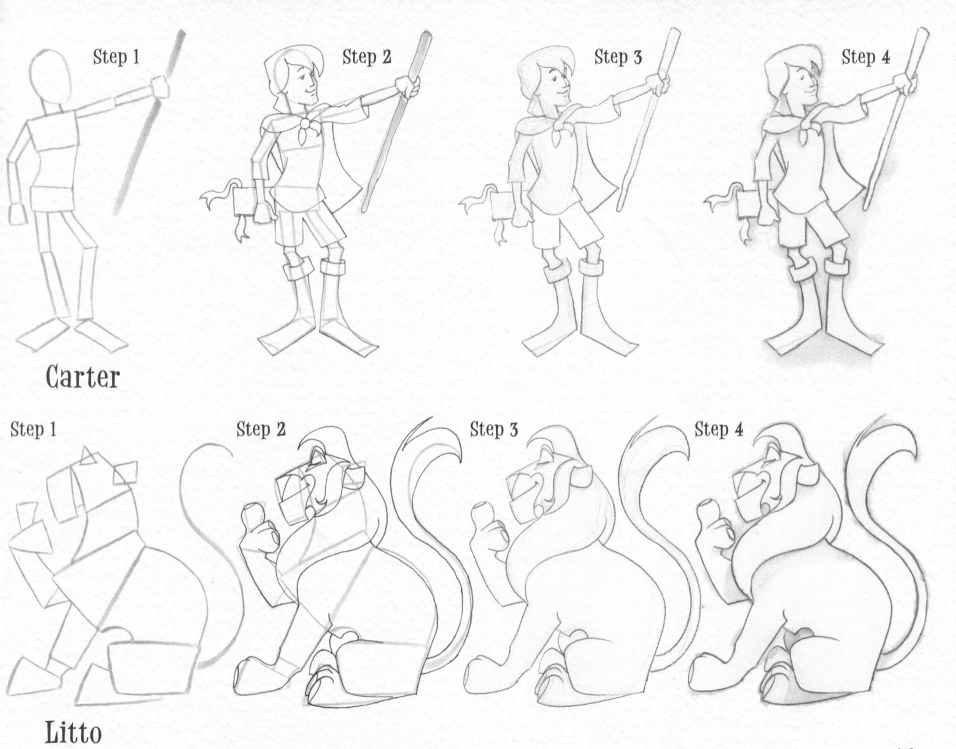

Step 1   Step 2   Step 3   Step 4

Carter

Step 1   Step 2   Step 3   Step 4

Litto

46

"The greatest treasure is your story.
What role will YOU play?"